Gitchi Gumee

Written by Anne Margaret Lewis
Illustrated by Kathleen Chaney Fritz

Mackinac Island Press

for the love of reading

To my husband, Brian, who always makes
me strive to do my best.

Anne Margaret Lewis

To my husband, John Fritz, for his expertise,
technical prowess and loving support.

Kathleen Chaney Fritz

First Edition

Library of Congress Cataloging-in-Publication Data

Lewis, Anne Margaret and Chaney Fritz, Kathleen

Gitchi Gumee
Summary: Gitchi Gumee (big water) shares his many moods and faces with a
young boy (Oshikinawe), and teaches him how to safely sail his vast waters.

ISBN 0-9749145-9-2

Fiction

10 9 8 7 6 5 4 3 2 1

Printed and bound in Canada by Friesens, Altona, Manitoba.

A Mackinac Island Press, Inc. publication
Traverse City, Michigan

www.mackinacislandpress.com

Gitchi Gumee

Three important words for this story~

GITCHI GUMEE [gitch-ē gü-mē] big water
OSHIKINAWE [ō-shē-ki-naü-ē] young boy
ININI [i-nin-ē] man

I am the great GITCHI GUMEE

with giant waves that prowl.
Along the sandy beaches,
I roar and swoosh and growl.

"Who dare to cross my mighty swells
that roll from shore to shore?
Who dare not heed the warning
I give before a storm?

For I am GITCHI GUMEE,
BIG water of many faces.
I reach about the endless land
with guests from many places."

"Gitchi Gumee," a young boy called my name.
"Gitchi Gumee," rolled off his lips.
"May I sail across your mighty waves,
   through your windy waves that whip?"

He sat there near his sailboat
upon the sandy shore,
waiting for my big fierce growl
to become a softer roar.

"What is your name?" I bellowed to the boy.
He stood there in soft silence.
"I will call you OSHIKINAWE."
Still...he was silent, shy, and tense.

"What is Oshikinawe?"
the boy whispered to me then.
I replied, "It's the name the Great Spirit gives
before young boys grow into men."

"I'm ready to cross you," said Oshikinawe,
with his boyish big brown eyes.
"Is it safe, Gitchi Gumee?" he asked.
"And if not, I must ask...WHY?"

"*Dear boy...*

...I AM THE GREAT GITCHI GUMEE,
big water of many faces.
I have been around for many years
and was formed from melted glaciers.

I know you want to venture out,
but there is much to learn and know.

Have patience, Oshikinawe...

...as you grow, you'll learn
and as you learn, you'll grow.

I will guide you in your passage
to test my mighty swells.
Watch and listen closely
and you will know my faces well.

Come with me now, Oshikinawe;
I will teach you how to sail.

Remember though...

...it will take many years of practice
for you to grasp my windy gales."

"Do you see my face
smiling on many days,
children playing among my beaches,
jumping through my gentle waves?

I compose myself for each new day
and stretch my morning yawn.
I ripple gently upon the shore
to invite the graceful dawn."

"Families marvel at my stunning beauty
as the sun calmly says 'goodnight.'
Fishermen fish big Gitchi Gumee,
as the weather plays just right."

"I **puff** my cheeks and **blow** my wind,

I tell my waves to wake.
I whip them to a frothy foam,
like frosting on a cake.

Sailors sail my windy gales,
dashing through my wild waves.
They cruise from coast to coast
on my windy blustery days."

"Freighters move across my foggy face;
Gitchi Gumee starts to stir.
Pines along the edge of Gitchi Gumee
start to bend and twist and whir."

"I will cradle you in my tender care
to guide you through this storm.

Oshikinawe…

…you must see my mighty powers
to gain the wisdom to explore.

The clouds above me swarm together
with darting lightning bolts.
Rain begins to pellet down,

then BOOM

…the THUNDER ROLLS!

Still…

…many shipwrecks lie beneath me;
they become a fishy haven.
Oshikinawe…I tell you…
…many freighters have been taken."

"Gitchi Gumee,"
    the boy called out~

"What about winter?
 Do you hibernate like a bear?
 Do you sleep all winter long,
 without a winter care?"

"Yes and no," I replied.
"Have you seen my winter face?
 I look like Old Man Winter
 in my snowy, frozen state."

"Children glide upon my

glistening ice,

so frozen close to shore.
They play among my icy caves,
with my growl a softer roar.

Each year I show my powers
when the seasons quickly change.
I rest my shoreline waves in winter...
...it's my Gitchi Gumee game."

"My ice begins to creak and crack,
my ice caves slowly thaw.
I will flaunt a brand new face,
to look upon with awe!"

"Gitchi Gumee...

...now that I have seen your faces,
I believe I understand;
Oshikinawe's life,
is in Gitchi Gumee's hands.

For YOU are the GREAT Gitchi Gumee,
with giant waves that prowl.
I respect your many faces
that roar and swoosh and growl!

You've taught me to sail your waters,
skimming along your sandy shore.
I have waited for your big fierce growl
to become a softer roar.

I have seen the warning signs
you give before a storm.

Gitchi Gumee ∼

You have shown me stormy waters,
my sail now tired, tattered, and torn."

"I will spread the message that you send
to respect and know your faces.
I will spread it throughout the endless land,
to your guests from many places."

"Gitchi Gumee thanks Oshikinawe,
so young and wise and brave.
Now you've discovered my many faces
ININI... MAN...
...is now your name!"